# The SWEETWATER RUN

## The Story of Buffalo Bill Cody and the Pony Express

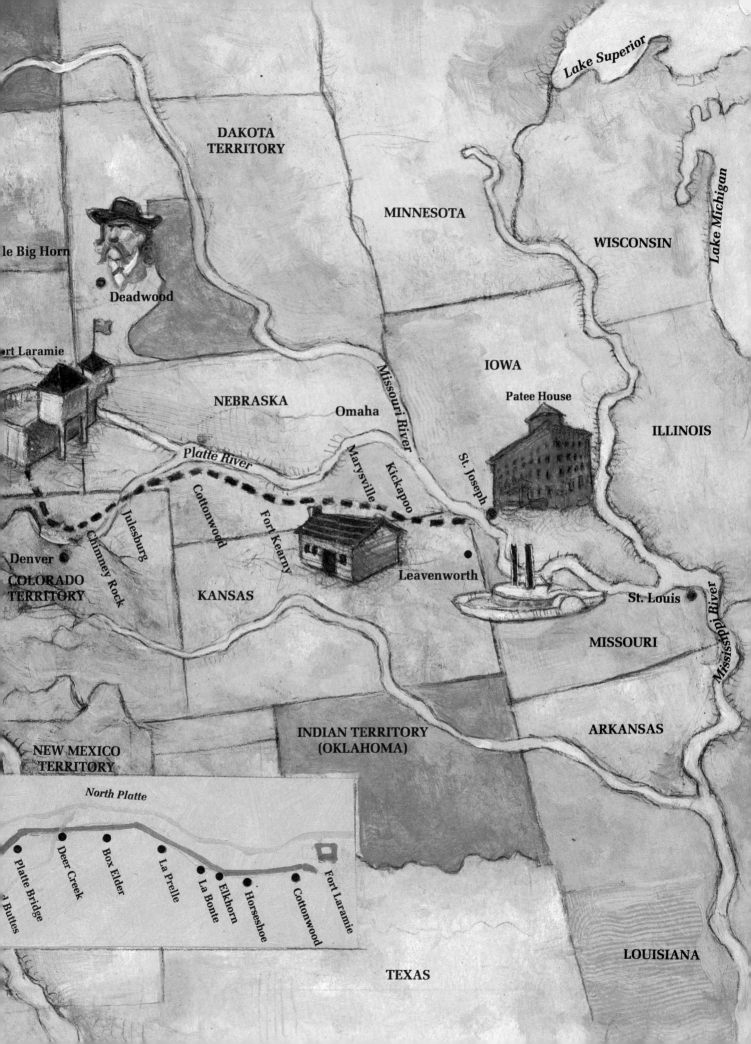

Lake Superior

DAKOTA TERRITORY

MINNESOTA

WISCONSIN

Lake Michigan

le Big Horn

Deadwood

IOWA

ort Laramie

Patee House

ILLINOIS

NEBRASKA

Omaha

Missouri River

St. Joseph

Platte River

Marysville

Kickapoo

Cottonwood

Julesburg

Fort Kearny

Denver

Chimney Rock

Leavenworth

St. Louis

COLORADO TERRITORY

KANSAS

MISSOURI

Mississippi River

NEW MEXICO TERRITORY

INDIAN TERRITORY (OKLAHOMA)

ARKANSAS

North Platte

Platte Bridge

Deer Creek

Box Elder

La Prelle

La Bonte

Elkhorn

Horseshoe

Cottonwood

Fort Laramie

Buttes

LOUISIANA

TEXAS

# The SWEETWATER RUN

## The Story of Buffalo Bill Cody and the Pony Express

Andrew
Glass

A Picture Yearling Book

Published by
Bantam Doubleday Dell Books for Young Readers
a division of
Bantam Doubleday Dell Publishing Group, Inc.
1540 Broadway
New York, New York 10036

**Visit us on the Web!**
**www.bdd.com**

**Educators and librarians, visit the**
**BDD Teacher's Resource Center at**
**www.bdd.com/teachers**

ISBN: 0-440-41186-6
Reprinted by arrangement with Doubleday Books for Young Readers
Printed in the United States of America
November 1998
10 9 8 7 6 5 4 3 2 1

to my father

In the spring of 1860 I was thirteen years old. That's when I first saw the notice posted around Fort Laramie of a mail service between St. Joseph, Missouri, and Sacramento, California. It was after Papa died, so I was helping support my mama and sisters. Twenty-five dollars a week was a darned sight more than I earned carrying messages between wagon trains.

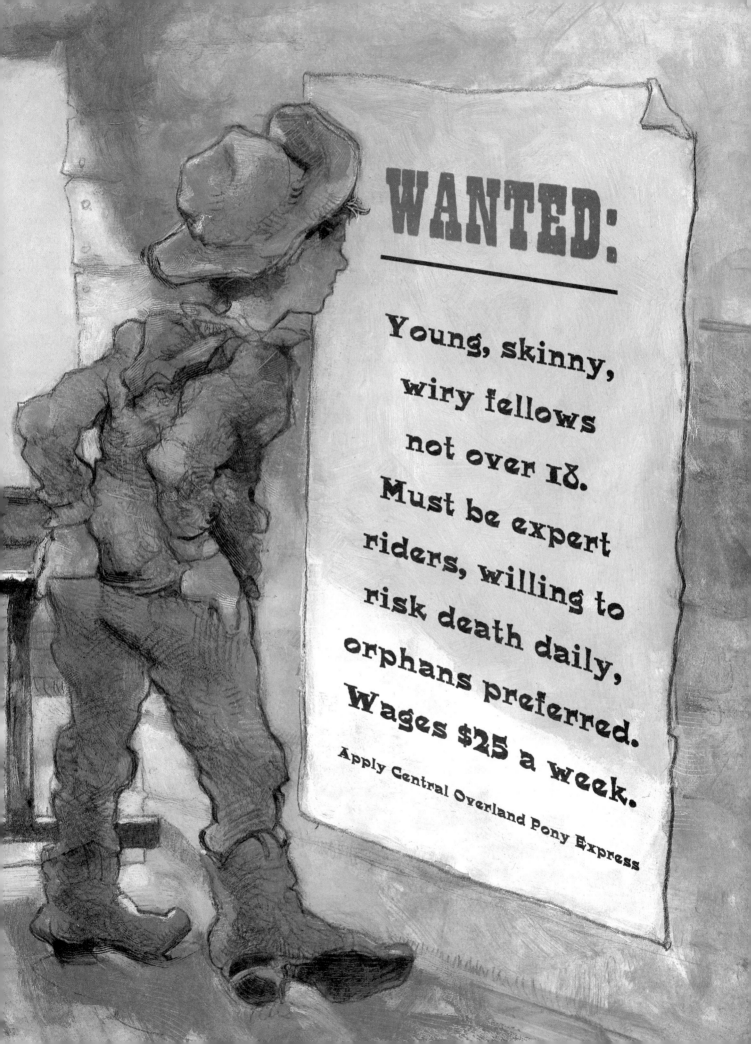

I got a ride thirty-six miles to the division headquarters at Horseshoe Station. They called the chief The Terrible Slade, 'cause folks said he'd as soon shoot ya as look at ya.

"I reckon yer puny enough, boy," Mr. Slade said, "but we ain't lookin' for youngsters to ride for the Pony Express. Now get along home to yer mama."

Luckily Bill Hickok, who'd already been hired, was playing poker in the corner. "Just hold on a minute, Slade," he said in his quiet way. "I worked with Will on the wagon trains out of Leavenworth. He's a lad knows how to do a day's work for a day's wages." Bill always spoke softly, but even tough guys like Mr. Slade listened.

"Well, I reckon I've got a run for ya, boy," said Mr. Slade. "I call it the *sweat and water run*. It goes like this. First off, you see to it there's a fresh pony ready for the company rider. The pony he leaves behind will be wore out and parched to the bone. You rub the sweat off the pony's hide and see he has plenty of water. That's why I call it the *sweat and water run*. Twenty dollars a month is what we're paying stablehands, son. Take it or leave it," he growled.

I was sorely disappointed, but I said, "I'll take it!" Right on the spot Mr. Slade hired me. I signed the company pledge, promising to live a clean, wholesome life, and received a company Bible.

"Irregardless of what's wrote on that there pledge," snarled Mr. Slade, "the most important rule is this: The mail must go through." He jabbed his big forefinger hard into my chest. "No excuses!"

I worked the Deer Creek Station, run by Mr. and Mrs. Boyd. I tended those ponies like royalty. Day or night I always had one saddled and ready. If exchanging a pony took more than two minutes, Mr. Boyd said I was lollygagging, and I won't even tell you what Mr. Slade called it. I bunked behind the stable so as to do my job the best I could.

One chilly November morning in 1860 I threw off my heavy buffalo blanket. "Today's the day," I said to my own big white horse, Old Mountain. The presidential election was over. Mr. Boyd figured it'd take three days to count the votes back East. Senator Gwin wanted the news in California inside of ten days. That very morning a Pony Express rider—a pony boy— was racing toward California, carrying the winner's name.

It'd be locked tight in the *mochila*, which is what we called the mail pouch.

Some folks said California was too far from Washington to be part of the same country. The pony boys were going to prove them wrong.

That morning, as I saw to my chores, I felt as jumpy as if I was making the run myself. I ran my hands over every bone and muscle of the best mare. Then I went around to the Boyds' for breakfast.

"This here's the way we learn what sorta country we're going to live in, Will," said Mr. Boyd. He smeared a lump of butter onto his griddlecake. "Slave or free."

"They say slavery is likely to pull our country apart," I replied.

"If Abe Lincoln is our new president, it's sure he won't tolerate a country half slave and half free," said Mrs. Boyd.

"Nope, not after all his abolitionist speechifying," said Mr. Boyd. "We could be headed for civil war if it's Abe Lincoln's name locked up in the *mochila*."

With a mouth full of mushy griddlecake and dried fruit, I asked, "Jake'll know who won when he rides in for a fresh horse, won't he?"

"I expect. So when you finish tending his pony, hightail it in here and tell us who the new president is," Mrs. Boyd ordered.

After breakfast I rode up the trail. I strained my eyes along the horizon. There was no sign of Jake. Considering all the natural hazards of the trail, not to mention Indians and bandits, the pony boys were downright punctual. But why did Jake have to pick this morning to be late?

"Here he comes!" I cried when I saw the dust cloud rising along the prairie. Soon I could see that Jake leaned unsteady in his saddle. I grabbed the fresh mustang's bridle and spurred Old Mountain to a full gallop.

Jake caught up and rode alongside. His buckskin pants were ripped open to the thigh. A bandanna was tied tight above his knee.

"The trail is clear!" he shouted. "Only I been snake-bit. I sucked it clean as best I could, but I'm riding no farther. You get the mail through to Three Crossings."

I pulled the mare to a standstill. "Mr. Slade ain't gonna like it," I said.

"What Mr. Slade ain't gonna like is the excuses you'll be giving him for why the mail sat around while you searched for a bona fide, official company rider."

I well remembered Mr. Slade's big forefinger poking me hard in my chest.

I jumped off Old Mountain and tossed Jake the reins.
"You take him in, and tell Mr. Boyd I'll get back soon as I can,"
I said as I swung myself onto the fresh mustang's back. Jake
tossed me the *mochila*, which I lashed tight to the saddle horn.
I took off and rode, like I was flying.

After ten miles the pony was pretty near spent and I was more hanging on than riding.

Just outside Red Buttes, a rider began galloping down the trail toward the station, leading a mustang alongside. When I came abreast I saw the rider was just a girl with pigtails. She was even younger than me.

Side by side we raced along. I stared hard at the new mustang. I'd never actually, personally made a jump at full gallop myself. Finally the girl shouted, "Is this gonna take all day, boy?"

I couldn't endure the scornful look in her eyes. "I'd do this *for* ya, boy," the girl yelled, "but my pa would tan my hide."

So I flipped the *mochila* across the mustang's empty saddle, took a deep breath, and threw myself over behind it. The girl grinned wide and tossed me the reins.

"Treat her good, miss. She ran her heart out for me,"
I called over my shoulder as the girl led my old pony away.
"You bet, boy!" she shouted.

"Here he comes!" townfolk shouted as I raced right past Red Buttes station. Somebody cried out, "Hey, pony boy, who won?" I was near to bustin' with pride. I shouted back, "I did—William Frederick Cody!" And that's the precise moment when I recollected the presidential election. Locked inside the *mochila*, lashed to my saddle, was the most important news since Paul Revere's ride. Without a key to open the pouch I couldn't find out who won. I couldn't shout the name like folks were expecting.

By Three Crossings it was almost dark. No one was waiting up the trail. I let out a loud coyote whoop and rode into the station. In the stable the station keeper's wife was hefting a saddle onto a fresh pony.

"Loyd's gone and got himself shot," she said. "In one afternoon he broke about every rule in that there pledge y'all signed. He drank alcohol, used foul language, gambled, and behaved in what you'd have to call a generally depraved manner. Then some other fool shot him, and there ain't no other rider neither. Guess you better ride, boy," she said, dropping the stirrup. "And, boy, who won the election?"

"I don't rightly know, ma'am," I replied.

I just leaped onto the pony and raced into the sunset.

Night fell clear. The sky lit up with stars and a bright full moon. The pony ran through the frosty air, like flying.

By moonlight I changed ponies at full gallop outside
South Pass, like I'd done it a thousand times.

Just nine miles out of Big Bend Station, a band of Sioux
charged out of a sandy ravine and chased me across the plain.
Bullets and arrows whizzed by my head. I stretched out low
across my pony's neck and whispered in his ear, "Run like the
wind!" We galloped hell-for-leather until I heard "Here he
comes!"

At Big Bend Station I slid from the saddle, limp as a rag. "The trail's not clear," I gasped.

Mr. Slade looked me up and down. "Ain't you the Boyds' stablehand?" he growled. Without waiting for a reply, he unlashed the *mochila* and hurried into the station house. When he came back out, with the mail for Sacramento and San Francisco, he knew whose name was locked inside.

He tossed me the *mochila* so hard, it nearly knocked me over. "How do ya feel, boy?" he asked roughly.

Wobbly as I was, I stood up as straight as I could and looked him in the eye. "Ready to ride," I answered.

"Okay, boy," he replied gruffly. "Yer gonna get yer chance. You and Abe Lincoln!" He grabbed the *mochila* and handed it to a fresh rider, who galloped off without a word.

"But not today," Mr. Slade snorted. "From now on, Will Cody, you'll be making the run from Red Buttes to Three Crossings. I think we'll call it the Sweetwater Run."

I rode the Sweetwater Run for those first bitter months of the War Between the States. Then the telegraph lines went through in 1861 and connected the East and the West in the blink of an eye.

After that I went back to working the wagon trains. Finally I joined up to fight against slavery as a scout in the Seventh Kansas Regiment.

The West changed after the war, and I admit now it was some of my doing. I hunted buffalo to feed the men who built the railroad. Folks came to call me Buffalo Bill. Soon the vast wilderness where I'd grown up could be crossed easily by rail. Settlers came with their families and built homes on the plains. Sometimes I felt I'd started a prairie fire that raged out of control. By the 1870s buffalo hunting was a gentleman's sport; then it became a slaughter. When the buffalo were all but gone, the Indians were defeated. The Wild West vanished like a dream, or like a pony boy racing across the plains.

Stories of the Pony Express caught the imagination of the whole world. I became a showman and built my Wild West Show on the spirit of the frontier, sharing the adventure of the days when the pony boys rode a wild relay race across the wilderness for the love of our nation. The Pony Express lasted only sixteen months, but when I think back to the proudest time of my life, I recall the days I rode the Sweetwater Run.

# Notes

The Pony Express was born in the imagination of Senator William H. Gwin of California. Gwin's idea was to speed urgent messages from St. Joseph, Missouri, to Sacramento, California, by organizing a relay race of expert riders on first-class horses. He convinced a successful freight company executive named William H. Russell to take on the ambitious project. Both of Mr. Russell's partners, a Mr. Majors and a Mr. Waddell, thought it was much too hazardous and expensive an undertaking to be profitable. Senator Gwin convinced them that once the service was up and running, the government would supply a mail contract to make it worth their while. However, by October 1861, when the Pony Express was disbanded, the firm of Russell, Majors, and Waddell was indeed bankrupt.

Russell announced that the Pony Express would make its first run by April 3, 1860. He had sixty-five days to get ready. Eighty skilled horsemen were chosen from hundreds of applicants. Most weighed less than 120 pounds. They signed an oath promising not to use profane language, drink alcohol, or fight, at least among themselves. Each was given a Bible. Their pay ranged from $50 to $150 per month plus room and board, high wages for the time.

The Pony Express purchased several hundred horses. East of Nebraska, most were Kentucky and Missouri stock; to the west, they were tough mustangs. They were cared for like racehorses and fed a rich diet of grain so that they could outrun grass-fed Indian ponies. Their lightweight saddles were specially made. At first each rider carried a Colt revolver as well as a carbine to protect himself and the mail. But soon the pony boys decided that the weapons were too heavy and that their fast ponies were their best defense.

One hundred ninety relay stations were set up over 1,966 miles of prairie, mountain, and desert. Each station had a corral and a barn. Riders, station keepers, and their helpers slept under buffalo robes on long wooden bunks or on packing crates. Home stations were set up every 75 to 100 miles as places for riders to rest. Stations were often dangerously far from settlements. Sometimes keepers and their assistants died defending them.

A relay station employed one keeper and one stablehand. Their duty was to have a fresh horse saddled before a rider arrived. Stablehands could see a rider coming by watching for the rising dust or by listening for distant hoofbeats. At night a rider signaled by whooping like a coyote. A rider flung his *mochila,* a leather pouch with four locked compartments called *cantinas,* to the keeper, who plopped it over the saddle of the fresh mount. The rider dismounted and shouted whether or not the trail he'd just ridden was clear of bandits and Indians. Then he leaped onto the fresh horse and galloped off. The exchange often took no more than fifteen seconds.

A telegraph line joining Carson City, Nevada, to St. Joseph, Missouri, was completed on October 20, 1861. Just two days later, the Pony Express came to an end.

In its short life of sixteen months, the Pony Express carried 37,753 letters on a total of 308 runs over 616,000 miles and captured the imagination of the whole world. Only one mail pouch was lost.

On April 3, 1860, a Pony Express rider started out from St. Joseph for Sacramento. At the same time, another Pony Express employee left Sacramento for St. Joseph, carrying mail in the opposite direction. Riding in relays, forty pony boys made their first east-to-west crossing in ten and a half days. Forty others took only ten days to travel from west to east. Before the Pony Express, a newspaper or letter, no matter how urgent, took twenty-five days to get from New York to San Francisco, traveling by wagon train or boat.

Once all the stations were running, riders averaged twelve miles an hour. The service was offered once a week at first, then twice a week. To keep weight to a minimum, letters were written on tissue and wrapped in oiled silk. Special lightweight newspapers were printed. The Pony Express delivery charge was five dollars per half ounce, payable in gold, so writers literally weighed their words.

Native Americans understood that messages carried by pony riders foretold the coming of more settlers to the plains. In just half a century, emigrants moving west had nearly trapped out the beaver and shot most of the buffalo that the plains tribes, the Sioux, Bannocks, and Cheyennes, depended on. Even coyotes were disappearing. Paiutes attacked and burned stations and ambushed riders along the route, disrupting service in May and June 1860. The harsh winter of 1860–61 slowed service until packmules were used to trample down the trail.

William Frederick Cody was born in Iowa on February 24, 1846. He had two older sisters and an older brother, who was killed in a riding accident. The family later moved west and settled in Salt Creek Valley, Kansas, about twenty miles from Fort Leavenworth.

When Will was seven years old, his father, Isaac Cody, was stabbed in the back while speaking against slavery. He survived, but the proslavery vigilantes who terrorized the territory continued to torment him. In April 1857, when his father died, eleven-year-old Will left school and began taking jobs to help support his mother and sisters. He worked as a messenger, riding between wagon trains departing from Fort Leavenworth. At Fort Laramie he met two famous mountain men, Kit Carson and Jim Bridger. They taught him the language of the Sioux, as well as sign language used by other tribes.

In 1860, when he was thirteen years old, Will asked Jack Slade, the division superintendent at Horseshoe Station, for a job with the Pony Express. The superintendent was known as The Terrible Slade because of his reputation for shooting people who disagreed with him.

Will proved himself one of the ablest and most colorful riders in the history of the Pony Express. He was said to have outrun Indians who ambushed him and to

have made a 320-mile run in twenty-one hours and forty minutes, replacing a rider who had been killed in a drunken brawl.

When the Pony Express ended, Will went back to working the wagon trains. At the age of eighteen, he was drawn into the Civil War. After he married Louisa Frederici, he worked as a buffalo hunter and a scout. His life was changed forever by a writer of dime novels named Ned Buntline. Will became famous overnight as Buffalo Bill Cody. Although he was now a celebrated showman and an actor, he dreamed of a show that would recapture the Wild West of his boyhood.

In 1882 Will organized *The Old Glory Blow Out.* He hired a few Native Americans and bought an old stagecoach. Using local cowboys, he reenacted a stagecoach robbery. There were shooting contests and a small herd of buffalo. The show was a sensation and gave him the inspiration for a bigger and better one. *Buffalo Bill's Wild West Show* opened in Omaha, Nebraska, on May 17, 1883. It became a hugely successful, rowdy extravaganza that toured the country. Will enlarged the original show, adding a Pony Express act during which a rider galloped into the ring, tossed a *mochila* to another rider, and raced off. The sharpshooter Annie Oakley joined the show as the first act, and the celebrated Sioux chief Sitting Bull became its main attraction. In 1887 the show went to London; soon it toured Europe. Buffalo Bill Cody became one of the best-known Americans of his time and helped to create the myth of the Old West.

Will Cody died January 10, 1917, at the age of seventy-one, in Denver. More than eighteen thousand people marched in his funeral parade. He was buried on Lookout Mountain, overlooking the city of Denver.

In this fictional account, my intention was to write a story that expresses the thrill of taking part in the great adventure called the Pony Express. Although there is no shortage of information about the Pony Express, it is difficult to separate fact from fiction. When the enterprise went bankrupt, most of its records were destroyed. The Patee House Museum in St. Joseph, home of the Pony Express Historical Association, was an invaluable resource.

It's probable that Division Chief Slade did give Will Cody the run from Red Buttes to Three Crossings, though Will may or may not have started as a stablehand. Wild Bill Hickok was indeed a friend of Will's and may well have spoken up for him, since Hickok also worked for the Pony Express. Wild Bill went on to become one of the most famous lawmen in the Old West. He toured with Buffalo Bill from 1872 to 1873. Hickok was shot in the back in Deadwood, Dakota Territory, in 1876, while playing poker. The Boyds are fictional, but many shared their strong feelings about the election of 1860 and concern over what it meant for the future of America.

The Pony Express carried the news of Lincoln's victory from Washington, D.C., to San Francisco in just seven days and seventeen hours. And, as the Boyds anticipated, Lincoln's election did change the course of history.

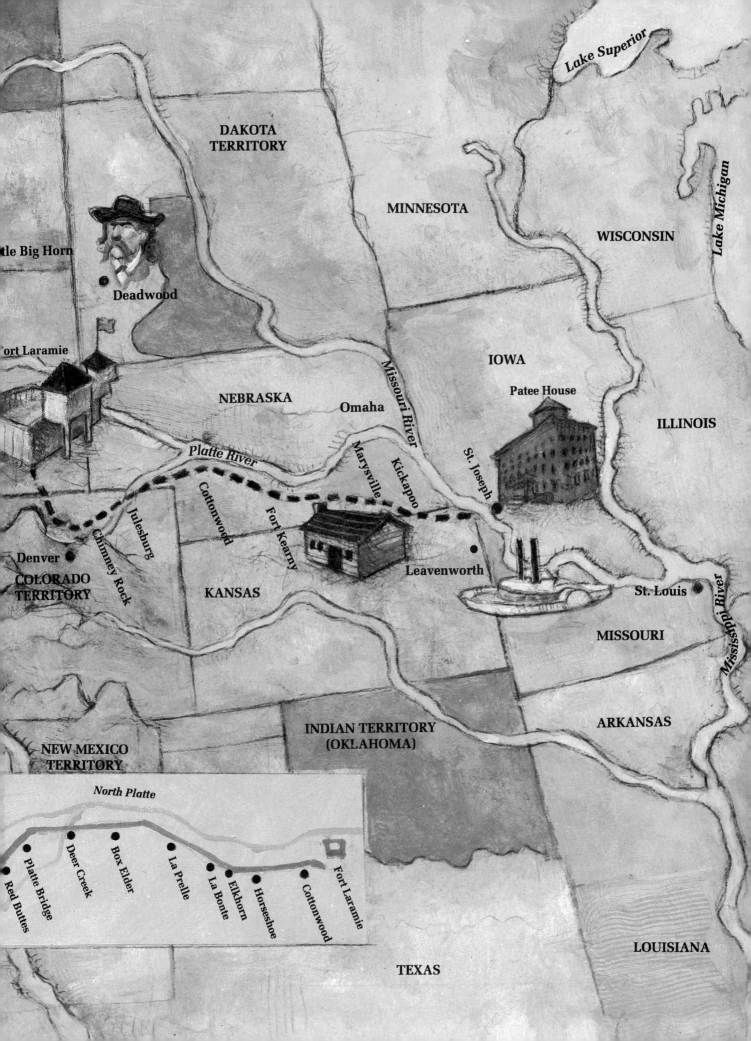

Lake Superior

DAKOTA
TERRITORY

MINNESOTA

WISCONSIN

Lake Michigan

tle Big Horn

Deadwood

IOWA

Patee House

ort Laramie

NEBRASKA

Omaha

ILLINOIS

Missouri River

Platte River

Marysville

Kickapoo

St. Joseph

Cottonwood

Fort Kearny

Julesburg

Chimney Rock

Denver

COLORADO
TERRITORY

KANSAS

Leavenworth

St. Louis

Mississippi River

MISSOURI

NEW MEXICO
TERRITORY

INDIAN TERRITORY
(OKLAHOMA)

ARKANSAS

North Platte

Platte Bridge

Red Buttes

Deer Creek

Box Elder

La Prelle

La Bonte

Elkhorn

Horseshoe

Cottonwood

Fort Laramie

LOUISIANA

TEXAS

**ANDREW GLASS** has written and illustrated several books for children, including *Folks Call Me Appleseed John* and *Bad Guys: True Stories of Legendary Gunslingers . . . of the Wild West*. He has also illustrated many books, including *Soap! Soap! Don't Forget the Soap!* and *She'll Be Comin' Round the Mountain* by Tom Birdseye, and the Spooky Books by Natalie Savage Carlson. He lives in New York City.